KNOCKS IN THE NIGHT

First North American edition Published by Starfish Bay Children's Books in 2016
ISBN: 978-1-76036-011-5
Es klopft bei Wanja in der Nacht © Dressler Verlag – Imprint Ellermann, Hamburg 1985
Published by agreement with Dressler Verlag GmbH, Hamburg, Germany
Translated by David-Henry Wilson
Printed and bound in China by Beijing Shangtang Print & Packaging Co., Ltd
11 Tengren Road, Niulanshan Town, Shunyi District, Beijing, China

Knocks in the Night

By Tilde Michels
Illustrated by Reinhard Michl

★★ STARFISH BAY
CHILDREN'S BOOKS

In a distant land of sleet and snow,
Where icicles hang and cold winds blow,
Beside the forest, closed up tight,
Stands Peter's house, all draped in white.

A storm now breaks in darkest night,
And Peter wakes up in a fright.
He's heard a sound he can't ignore.
"Who's that knocking on my door?"

Straight to the door he has to go,
And finds a hare out in the snow,
Shivering, quivering, coughing, sneezing.
"Please let me in. I'm f-f-freezing!"

Peter says, "Come out of the storm.
I'll light the stove to get you warm."
The crackling flames flicker and dart,
Warming the body and the heart.

The house is still. The little hare
Curls up snugly in the chair.
Peter settles down for the night.
"Pleasant dreams, friend hare, sleep tight."

But hardly have they closed their eyes
When there's another loud surprise.
Peter must go and see who knocks,
And is confronted by a fox.

"I'm frozen," he says, "from top to toe.
I've had enough of storm and snow.
I really don't know what to do,
So may I spend the night with you?"

"Oh no!" the hare cries out in fear.
"Please don't let the fox in here!
Foxes have a nasty habit
Of eating things that look like rabbit."

The fox, still shaking like a jelly,
Replies despite his empty belly,
"I swear by all that's good and true
I shall not lay a tooth on you."

"You've promised now, so don't forget it,"
Peter says, "or you'll regret it."

The house is still. They all retire.
The fox curls up beside the fire.
Peter settles down for the night.
"Pleasant dreams, friend fox, sleep tight."

But once again — it's quite absurd —
All kinds of noises can be heard.
Thumpy bumpy! What's out there?
The answer is a big brown bear.
And what is more, if truth be told,
His teeth are chattering with the cold.

Peter has a good long stare.
"Where can I put a big brown bear?"

The fox's fear is plain to see.
"This will be the end of me.
The bear is simply sure to know
That it was just two weeks ago
I robbed him of a juicy steak,
So now revenge he'll want to take."

Despite his frozen eyes, nose, ears,
The brown bear senses all these fears
And swears — no matter what's been done
—
He really won't hurt anyone.

"OK," says Peter, "but be good!"
And on the fire he throws some wood.

The house is still. Bear in the corner,
Warm as a sausage in a sauna.
Peter settles down for the night.
"Pleasant dreams, friend bear, sleep tight."

Meanwhile, the snowflakes keep on tumbling.
The wind keeps howling, roaring, rumbling.
The strongest trees are bending, breaking.
The little house is shivering, shaking.
But everyone inside sleeps tight
Till morning drives away the night.

But as the light spreads all around,
The hare's heart begins to pound.
"The fox is foxy as can be.
He's much too dangerous for me.
I'm not daft, and I'm not dumb.
I can hear his grumbling tum.
The best thing I can do is go."
So out he hops into the snow.

The fox wakes up and sniffs the air.
At first, he doesn't see the bear,
But suddenly, he spots his error,
And all his body shakes with terror.
"The bear will never be my friend.
This tale will have a tragic end.
If I'm not careful, he'll soon catch me.
Then he'll do much more than scratch me."
Before the bear can say hello,
The fox is slinking through the snow.

Snug in his corner, the bear's asleep,
Snoring loudly, long and deep.
He's thawed all over during his doze.
He can waggle his ears and twitch his nose.
Even his fur coat's nice and dry.
He grunts and yawns and opens an eye,
But then a scream he can barely stifle:
On the wall is a hunting rifle.

"Oh no, a safe place this is not.
I'd better leave before I'm shot.
Out there the sun is warm and red.
In here I'll end up cold and dead!"
And so, as quietly as a mouse,
The big bear tiptoes from the house.

Peter finally opens his eyes
And looks around with great surprise.
The room's quite empty. It would seem
The night of knocks was just a dream!

Outside in the morning glow,
Three sets of tracks run through the snow.

Peter's face is a sunny beam.
"Now I know it was not a dream.
Who'd believe it? Thanks to the weather,
We spent a night in peace together."

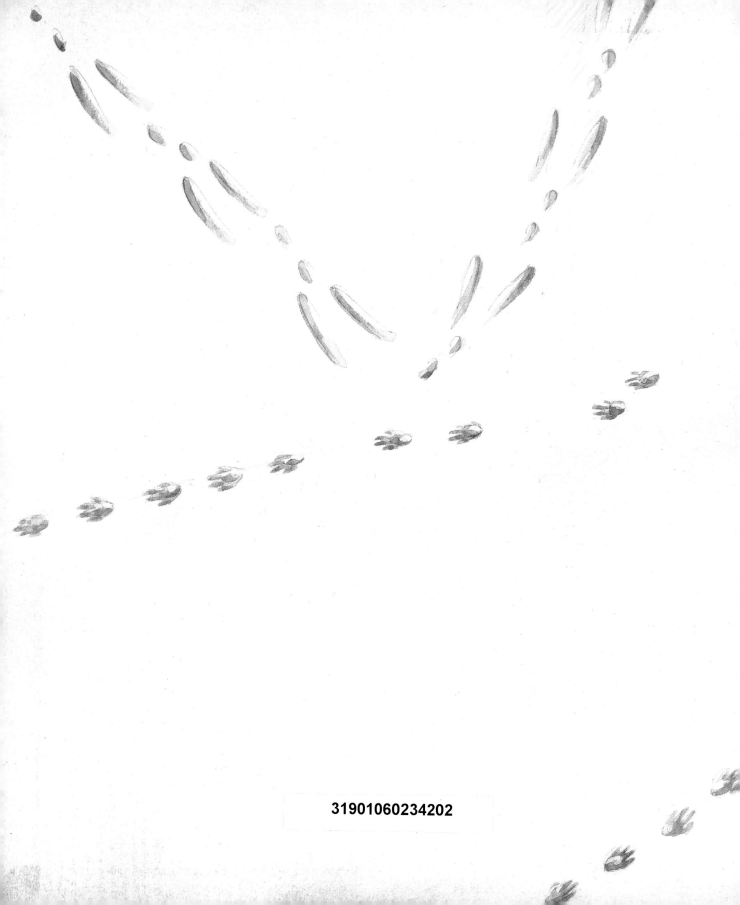